Night Wall

by Duncan Weller

Simply Read Books

Julie and her young cousin Sarah left their city homes of towering glass and steel and travelled north. Julie was hoping to escape for a while from what she called her busy cartoon life. Sarah was looking forward to their stay in a small cabin in the woods.

After a long journey they finally came to where the roads ended and the walking paths in the great forests began.

Soon after they arrived, Julie and Sarah set out to explore the woods. They found a path and followed it deep into the forest.

"I feel like I'm walking on the bottom of the ocean," Sarah said.

Later, Sarah sang along happily to her radio while she unpacked her things. She was thrilled to be on a big adventure. When night fell, Julie came to the room and asked her to turn off the music.

"Sarah, I want quiet now. It's time to get ready for bed."

Tucked into bed, Sarah closed her eyes and listened to the sounds of crickets and the wind whispering through the trees. She imagined climbing to the top of the tallest tree and becoming a bird that could fly over the forest in the starry night.

LARA WOOD
the boy from the
EMPERORS

Julie didn't like the woods at night. She roamed around the cabin nervously. When she looked out the windows, she saw moving shadows in the moonlight that shifted between the trees and imagined ghosts and leering monsters. Her sleep that night was restless and uneasy.

Early the next morning, Julie called a contractor from the nearest town. She told him that she wanted a wall built around the cabin.

The men from the construction company arrived early and set to work immediately. By the afternoon, the wall was almost finished.

Sarah brought some lemonade to the men. She liked how they called each other names such as Big Bear, Wolfman and Wildcat. One of the men said to Sarah, "You need a wall like I need a bad toothache."

"I don't want the wall," said Sarah, "Julie does."

The man frowned and went back to work.

The wall was up. The sun fell behind the trees. It was the blue hour before sunset.

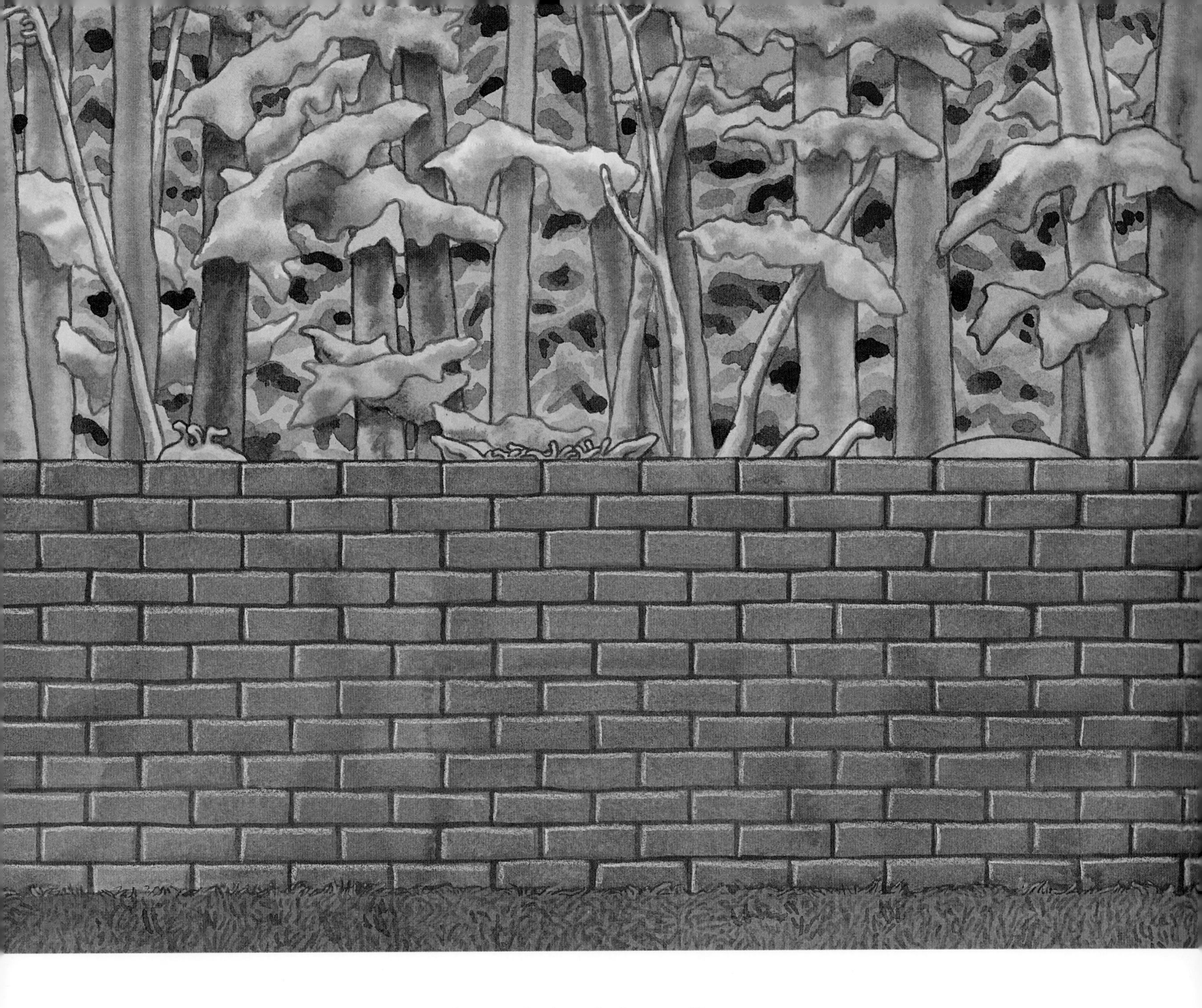

In that magical hour, in the forest behind the wall, strange creatures began to appear.

When Sarah passed the living room window, what caught her eyes made her yell in surprise, "LOOK! LOOK! LOOOOOK!"

Julie took one look at the creatures and jumped in fright. She quickly grabbed two brooms, gave one to Sarah and cried, "We have to get rid of them! They have to go away!"

"They look just like cartoons," Sarah said. "They don't look so scary."

Sarah ran outside and Julie followed. Swinging their brooms wildly, they screamed at the creatures, "GO AWAY! SHOOO! GET OUT OF HERE!"

They managed to chase the creatures away from the wall, or so it seemed, for when they got back inside the cabin, they looked out the window and...

... the creatures had returned, but there were more of them.

Julie and Sarah ran out again, but this time ...

... the creatures climbed over the wall, and ...

... lurched into the backyard.

Julie quickly locked all the doors and windows. Then she called the contractor and said firmly, "The wall doesn't work. We've got monsters in our backyard. You've got to take the wall down – tonight!" There was a pause. "Okay, then first thing tomorrow morning. I want that wall down!"

Sarah stayed close to Julie while the creatures surrounded the cabin.

"It looks like a circus out there," said Sarah, taking a peek out the window. "Do you think they're real?"

"Of course they're real." Julie answered. "You see them, don't you?"

One by one, as the sun rose, the creatures climbed back over the wall and disappeared into the forest.

The construction crew arrived in the morning and took down the wall. The men enjoyed smashing it to pieces.

After they left, Sarah begged Julie to take a walk with her in the forest, telling her, "The monsters are gone. Let's go! It's okay now." She added, "The forest is so beautiful. You'll see for yourself."

Julie was apprehensive but finally agreed to go with Sarah into the forest. Along the wooded path something caught Julie's attention. Moving closer, she discovered a small violet chest, partly hidden in the vines and ferns.

Sarah ran to the chest and opened it. "Look! Look!" she cried with delight. Julie knelt down beside Sarah.

Inside the chest were all the creatures from the previous night, in the form of tiny, brightly painted figurines.

"They're so small," said Julie.

"See – they're not so scary," said Sarah, smiling.

That afternoon, Julie took a nap after lunch. She slept peacefully while Sarah brought out her plasticine and modelling tools and made her own monster.

The day arrived when it was time to go home. They headed south, taking the chest with them.

"I'll miss the forest," said Sarah.

"We'll come back again soon," promised Julie.

They would often return to the cabin in the forest, but never again would the monsters leave the violet chest. From then on, the monsters remained very small.

INVOCATION
to the
MUSES

Published in 2005 by Simply Read Books Inc. **www.simplyreadbooks.com**

Cataloguing in Publication Data

Weller, Duncan, 1965-
Nightwall / Duncan Weller, author and illustrator.

ISBN 1-894965-13-2

I.Title.

PS8645.E45N53 2005 jC813'.6 C2004-902882-0

Printed in China *10 9 8 7 6 5 4 3 2 1*

Book Design by Elisa Gutiérrez *Jacket Design by Duncan Weller*

Colour Scans by ScanLab